MISS

A TALE OF ADOLSCENT LOVE

SHIVAKUMAR UPAVASI

Copyright © Shivakumar Upavasi
All Rights Reserved.

INTORDUCTION

MISS

SHIVAKUMAR UPAVASI

A TALE OF ADOLSCENT LOVE

Published by Notion Press Chennai

Copyrights: Author

7022167791,supavasi@rediffmail.com

In my adolescence a young lady's beauty had a great impact on my mind. At that age I was not so matured to understand the women's beauty, but it continued for my lifetime. So, I want to share my memories of her beauty in the form of this book. It will be my contribution to her beauty and nothing else to do with her personal life. Moreover it will be a way or means to thank her who had made me the author.

Beginning

It was Wordsworth who wrote about Lucy; The Solitary reaper and Kalidasa wrote about Shakuntala in his work Abhinva Shakuntala and they are my great ideologies in life for writing about women. We Indians believe "Satyam, Shivam, Sundaram" that means where there is truth the God exists there and that thing is beautiful. So beauty is the real thing God has created in all his creations of both living as well as non living things.

If I was a candle

I would burn for a while

For enjoying your beauty.

It was in the evening there was no electricity and you lighted the candle. It started burning and it was me. The movement you lighted it; I was born and just watching your eyes. The eyes that have many complications in life and never compromise with anything and the love filled with infinity ; they are the blooming flowers they are the burning balls and infinite hearts they shall break ,they cheer in happiness and sustain tears in sorrow.

And after lighting it, you just started taking rest on the cot, just giving your fingers some work to scribble the head but the candle was watching your nose. The nose was so beautiful that there are no words to tell about it, still I try "Nose is guilty because it is the first sense organ to open human emotions, long and wide just attracted for a jolly ride, killed many men when it had movements, expressing the sovereignty of women especially the character of getting anger, I was a bit afraid but still I say it has the power to create love and lust in any of the average men, what I could have done?" *'Just born to burn and die.'*

You got up and opened the window some breeze was coming that you wanted to enjoy, I know when fan is not there you cannot sit in the room. The gentle flow of wind started disturbing me but I want to be still live for another 25 minutes. The velocity increased and I was in the threat that I may die, but you closed the window and saved me, 'thankyou dear'. You went near the Jesus Christ photo and saluted him and turned back, now I could see your figure you are lovely, beautiful and dashing; these are the words commonly used. Now I will tell about my feelings; You looked like the bride about to marry me in the church, so comfortable so happy that what would happen, if I could dance with you, hug you and kiss your lovely lips. I was just dreaming and my enemy entered the 'electricity'.
You just rushed to blow the candle but please give me another five minutes I shall vanish. But you are prepared to kill me and someone rang the calling bell and you just moved towards the door. Thankyou, God you saved me. After a while you returned and you were moving towards the candle to blow it but the phone rang .

I have just three minutes and I want to say that the beauty that costs my life, makes me burn and wants to die was just the true love that was more pure and more authentic in the world ; I shall have born in any form to watch your beauty ; Its time I shall die...

HER SMILE

The Smile that stopped my heart for a while;

As Egypt is the gift of the Nile;

My life survives for that lovely Smile.

When she recited something from her mouth;

Literally believe me, she killed the youth.

The tongue that tried to reach out the lips; waves of the sea all of a sudden
travel fast to hit the shore;

Teethes that sparkled with the whiteness of the sun and the brightness of
stars, budding my heart to bloom in love.

Her lower lips for that I do not have the words to fix; was he a fool who
painted the Monalisa's lips for years?

Until today my heart has been wounded by that gentle smile;

Quite natural; Both admirable and adorable for me;

Single smile and just like a missile; fired openly and victims were many
including me.

The way she laughs; the shy, the lie, the pride were hard to digest but her
innocence in the smile kills; then many a times I was born ; to burn , to
bloom and to write about the stunning beauty that made me so creative, so
energetic and so lonely to sit in a corner and write...........................

THE PHASE OF GLAMOUR

In the bright sunshine about 9.00 AM the lady walked all the way through
many hearts. She was the gift of God for all those eyes of males

irrespective of their age and jealousy for all the females. Those long thick hairs loading a handful of flowers; oiled and combed neatly that almost touched her lower abdominal. The watch in her left hand and the vanity bag lagging to her right shoulder; books in the right hand almost pressing the chest; lady walked with her usual smile.

If I was a honey bee then I would have collected nectar from her lips; pink and brown; broad and narrow; bitten by her own teethes and watered by her own tongue. Lips make her smile pretty but she was witty. The brown cheeks like the parts of a mango; cut as two slices; softer more than the silk. If I would have touched them then I could have written more. Just as the cheese; dry and plain and not even a single pimple could be found using a microscope. Those lovely cheeks joined to form the marvelous chin. Nose like carrot that redefined her beauty; pride, honor, intelligence and fulfilled the self attachment in a prescribed manner. It had anger and it had love; it was affectionate and more passionate towards the duty. At times she breathed heavily to give life to her healthy body. Her eyebrows were like a tiny grass on the mud of the flower pot; small and tiny hairs standing like children; one after another in the school prayer line. When the drops of the sweat did flow from her forehead to her eyes they stopped them. *If I was the drop of the sweat that travelled from her forehead to cheeks and the chin; I would be the luckiest than the God.* Eyes are more dominant; they will not compromise for anything; they are bold, filed with love and affection; they literally hate men and no one can talk with her; the eye contact as men fear, women bear and close associates never share the real experience. The strong teethes like the Himalayas protecting India; milky white; just strong and straight. They were like the diamonds arranged to glitter when she opened her smile. The broad forehead and the leafy ears; what still the creator should have added to disturb the generation of men?

The glamorous face and the body covered with Indian traditional sari and blouse; as the lady walked with books in hand believe me she killed males with the sound proof guns.

Her wide chest and those strong arms; personality was like a lady cop but still beautiful as an idol for the architect to carve in his own heart and the painter to paint in his own soul. Strong stem like thighs that were accompanied by the earth like feet, balancing the milestone of beauty; safer towards her destination.

Her postures were more crucial to watch and she denied all who tried to speak about her beauty. In hot afternoons she had some sweat and in cold winters there was a little cough. Just stayed and talked to the work limitations and didn't care anybody irrespective of age or gender. She loved to be alone and lonely and I did feared about the future. Infinite Love for small ones and respect for elders and tried to maintain a flexible distance with colleagues.

MY DREAM

With my arms widely stretched;

Wait for her to Just to come and hug

Until this hour I wait someone to meet

Was it my fate?

The roses shower their colour

to her pink and brownie lips;

The honey bees deposit honey on her lips

And the lovely breeze adds some mist to her cheeks.

In the first look she prisoned me in her heart

And survived me with her wine of beauty.

Lady's beauty that had a strong influence on my mind and soul; provokes me to write

I shall do it forever............................

IN THE CLASS

AS she starts explaining something, I just stared her without batting my eyelids for minutes together. She moved her hands and lips that scribbled my heart. Eyes said many things to me but at that age what I could have understood. Just a spectator; if once she stared at me I was clean bold just like Patrick Paterson breaking the stumps when had a wicket of the batsman. It was a joy for me to see her in the class and felt happy within my heart and I just could not say to anyone; it was adolescence and in what way I could have described about the lady that influenced me so much. The twinkling stars, the singing birds and the roaring clouds didn't have so much passion in them that I had to express about her at that time. The roses didn't had so much color to match her glamour; ornaments will fail to justify themselves if she wore them; dress are just useless to redefine the marvelous creature of beauty; she was the Goddess of Beauty for me and if someone thinks I have gone mad by writing such lines that is acceptable as it is deserved.

Every time I have to accept that whatever she explained in the class I didn't understood for the reason it was my possessiveness to watch her ;feel happy and enjoyed in such a way that it was meaningless, hopeless , hate less and quite madness. As she turned around to write something on the board then I felt as if someone robbed my happiness of watching her spectacular speech, the way she pronounced English; that face, that glamour, that caliber, that professionalism; I should admit to God that he should have not created her at least to ruin me so badly. When the bell rang she moved with the dust of chalk piece on her hands, but she didn't cared and any of the students followed her to ask something; she just warned to be in the class for the next period.

In the lunch hours if she went to office I just watched her sitting in the ground. For she was the exceptional:

The joy of all things is not equal to her single look;

For she was enriched with an angel's beauty

That God might have created for me; those fabulous eyes; lusty lips; fruity cheeks; naughty nose; jasmine eyes; tiny eyebrows; hairs thicker than the material of the bird's nest; figure was like the sculpture carved on the rocks; painted in the Ajanta Caves; the true beauty, the rare one, but one and the only one existing in the planet as per my viewpoint.

Not to take her name;

She is more pious

And at times I am guilty for expressing the maturing beauty

It buds in my heart and will bloom all my lifetime

She impressed a generation; heavenly creature and if human then God only should know as He is the creator.

I shall beg her for just a gentle smile;

That makes me happy for a while

Beauty that rose to create waves in the heart

Just defeat's the ego and bows the head in her feet

She may be human to others; but for me 'the Goddess' who filled joy, humor and thought lessons of beauty just by impression and not even a single expression; to be honest I never meant that no one was beautiful in that world but her beauty had a very sensational impact and I had been wounded until this hour.

On A Saturday

It was already late and I had to attend the prayer. I rushed with a great speed and parked my bicycle. Just moved to join the line, but the prayer started and I had to stand at least 100 yards from the prayer line. The school bag had fewer books and there was no lunchbox that day. I stood with the feeling that if the drill starts after prayer then I could join it. But all of a sudden I turned left someone is standing at a distance of 10 yards. She was my Goddess and I started worshipping her with all the dedication which was preserve for her beauty. I do not remember much but I shall try to analyze

Beside me she stands; the evergreen beauty

A bit tensed and a bit worried

The sharp teeth biting her lovely lips

Dress was yellow and the climate was bright

It was a sunny day, I was so lucky to stand so close to her and felt happier on that day

Let the jingle bells ring for her; clouds shower the yellow flowers; bees dance around her; birds salute her by forming a line in the sky, what all happens in front of me, but I was a spectator.

Can I have a chance to touch then, what I shall do?

Go and tell her about my feelings

If so; she would have slapped me

After all she was my teacher

The few minutes I have enjoyed standing by the side of her is enough for my life; if there is another life then I should have born;

For her in such a way;

A small rose in the flower pot

Kept in a window of her bedroom

As she poured water with her gentle

Hands, they made me alive to watch the beauty

I will be watching the beauty when

I will be a bud

And wait for the day to bloom

As a flower; to be a spectator to watch

The Stunning beauty

Today I have bloomed then she will pick me up;

Then I shall die

But I will be in her head;

Doesn't have life

I shall be born to watch the beauty many a times in any form to prove that she was the most beautiful women in my life

At last the prayer ended and she made her way to the office room and they were one of the best movements and now memories of life that I have been enjoying since decades.

THE PILL FOR THE ILL

On that day I was suffering from fever cough and cold but I had to attend the class for writing a unit test. It was after the interval almost third period and when I started to write the test. I wrote a few lines and just put my forehead to the desk and rested as it was not possible to write. My friend sitting next to me informed about the situation but I couldn't hear any sound. After that it continued for some time and a gentle hand started rubbing my head. I just got up and that hand touched my forehead to test the heat of the fever; the movement I was shocked and opened my eyes slowly; she was my Goddess of Beauty

In a single touch my heart stopped; murmured in my ear that the lifetime dream has been fulfilled; the ambitious boy was totally vanished in me; a small child now I want to be so that she carries me and I could sleep on her shoulder; everyone will kiss the small child and she may not be the exception; more ambitious; more curious; around me they gathered but nothing could be understood as she touched my chin and neck to test the fever; I just cannot explain; felt as if the storm carried me away with a great velocity destroying my body; all were asking me to go home and my eyes were just watching her; but I do not want to go home for I want to see her; talk to her and get sympathy for not feeling well.

Before she touched me; I was not feeling well; And after that touch I was ill of that beauty; the illness of her beauty that was like the scattered sunlight touched me physically, mentally and heartily as well as solely; In illness people take rest, contact their doctor; for me it was not like that; for cure I want to peep into her eyes; want to have a warm and long hug, prepare myself to be the fortunate if she just kissed my forehead; is it greed , lust, love crush etc? I do not have answer for the circumstances prevailing; accompanied by my friend to reach my bicycle and then reached home. I remembered the situation and fell ill of the stunning beauty and that illness continues at this hour also.......................................

ON ONE EVENING AFTER THE SCHOOL

We were playing football in the last period and the bell rang. It was the time to go home but I and my friend were still playing as we have brought our bags to go home. As we gave the ball and started going towards the gate. Someone

called me by name and it was a familiar voice. I just turned; all of a sudden; it was like a blow of thunder to my ears and it was my Goddess; as she moved towards me; my heart trembled, eyes squashed from that vision, lips dried as earlier as they could have; hands started shaking and she moved towards me; my heart just stopped a while as she came nearer to me. She just questioned 'Other day you were not feeling well no, are you okay?' I was just watching the way she opened the speech and my heartbeat started increasing rapidly and at a random there were multi changes in my body. Any way I collected all my energy just to say 'Yes Miss'. Then she walked away with that lovely smile. It was the first time that I have ever talked to her and believe me it was a great movement of joy and bliss ;losing her to watch as she moved fast towards her destination.

On that night I had a dream;

She scribbled my head

With her stiff fingers

I was sleeping on the bench

As I opened my eyes slowly

And raised my head to see her;

She gave some milk with her eyes

As they were milky white; honey with those lovely lips

And I was reborn many a times with that lovely smile;

Just floating in the sea of Joy; enjoying the women's beauty

Someone slapped me and then I came to know it was my dream.

THE UNEXPECTED RAIN

It was almost 1.30 in the afternoon we were having lunch and suddenly the rain started as we thought that it may take some time. All of a sudden all the students sitting in the ground ran to the classes and some even sat in the corridor for eating their lunch. I was in the classroom and just came out to wash my hands with the water bottle. She was standing and her clothes were wet a little and she was enjoying the climate.

The watered face and the wet clothes as the water drops made their way
from head to the marvelous chin, through the mango sliced cheeks. She
opened her hairs to get them dry as

Breeze disturbed them; they kissed her nose, lips, cheeks and chin; as she
tried to tie those long strong black hairs with her hands; the wet brownie
face as the hair oil from her head has made its way to her face with the
rain water; she was looking better with the oily face; open hairs; breeze
hugging her and kissing her; teethes just sparkling like sunrays; nose
inhaled some air often as she has become cold; the wet body and that
lovely sari; God should have thrown me to this earth when she was born ;
at least I had the sense or it was possible to give some colour to my
feelings as all know that the adolescence is like the temporary madness.

ON A SUNDAY

I was just returning from my friend's house after returning him the book
on a Sunday. As commonly Sunday is a holiday I was very slow on my
bicycle and stopped near a public tap to drink some water as already it was
10 o' clock; a bit heat of sun was there. As I was about to remove the stand
and ride the bicycle it was a wonderful scene and my eyes didn't believe
that my Goddess was just opposite to me. As she was in a rush to go
somewhere, but still managed to smile at me and moved very fast. I was
just happy like someone got water in the desert. The cream sari and the
black blouse as she moves; creates sensation among the eye of every male;
cheeks like the chocolate cake and lips like the kissan jam; eyes like butter;
body like the white bread; what a breakfast?

I fallowed her from a distance of 100yards and I came to know that she
was attending the prayer at the Church. I did not know about the church
and about the prayers commenced on Sundays was also not known by me.
But I had watched the movie Amar Akbar Anthony movie song in
Chitrahar where Amitab Bachan wears a decent coat and Zeenataman a
red frock in the song. I imagined myself in Amitsab's dress and my Godess
in that pink dress. Believe me she looked so pretty with that dress but she
was a bit fat than Zeenathaman as she was a handsome personality. Then I
remember that the weddings of Christians commences at the Church. I do

not remember in which movie I have seen the white frill frock of the bride and the black coat of the bridegroom as they have a ring ceremony and the Father will be reciting something when the marriage event happened. I just imagined the situation with her:

The white gown; the white gloves; the white veil tied like a crown on her head; she sparkled those white teeths; eyebrows scribbled like a cut rainbow; eyelids like the fish moved in the aquarium; lips like strawberry that were tasted by the tongue continuously; nose like a strong sword of a warrior that killed men literally; soft creamy cheeks and v-shape chin; sculpture of a dancing lady on a rock like the body physic; poet's poem; artist's drawing and my Goddess of beauty that God created for me.

I was just to put the ring someone disturbed me by slapping at my back. He was my old classmate Christian friend who came to see a girl near the Church. I just could not stand there when he entered the scene and gave some reason; just moved to my home.

THE CIRCUS

Those days circus was more popular and every year a circus company would come to our town. Normally people were more interested to watch it. On Sundays almost it was houseful. On that Sunday I and my relatives went to watch the circus. It started at 5 PM and we enjoyed a lot as the joker made the audience laugh by his tricks. After sometime I went outside to bring the popcorn and to my surprise my Goddess was coming inside with her colleagues. It was a movement of Joy and I just moved side as they entered into the scene. She and her colleagues took the tickets of sitting in front chairs which was costlier than the gallery. After she went and sat there she enjoyed a lot and I was watching her smiles not less than fifteen minutes. It was already half an hour she was in the circus. Normally she loves to eat as much as I know her and it was correct. She went to buy the popcorn and I gave some reason to my family members and just followed her. Normally she walks straight and least bothered about who walk around her. I maintained a distance and was watching her; today she was Very Special;

Her hairs were open and dry; ears decorated with the lovely ear rings; a small red bindhi to represent that area of breaking the wave like eyebrows; eyes full of shy and pride; the chocolate chudi and veil protecting the stiff chest and covering that lovely waist; open chappals; nose that all the way ruined men; What a beauty? If God have seen her in that appearance; all the way He would have travelled from heaven to earth to hug her; her seriousness, smile, shy, pride; believe me She was the Lucy of Solitary Reaper and today I remember those lines ' a violet by a mossy stone; half hidden from the eye' and 'a maid whom there were non to praise'; especially the lower lips claiming her possessiveness to hate men literally; figure like the art work carved in the stones of Badami; painted by Ravi Verma in his works; the movements encountered by any one's eyes never forget that she was not an human a celestial being; an angel to serve beauty from her all parts of body; the beauty of Godess; who is born for me.

As I watched her from a distance and thought that she will not notice me. It was my bad luck her eyes spotted that shy boy who was staring at his miss. All of a sudden when there was an eye contact; I just moved away as if I had no reason to stand there. She stopped a while and just moved away towards the circus tent. Somehow I have managed to escape from the scene but next day in the class I was arrested. She moved to me with some anger in her eyes and opened 'You, stand up, were you not in the circus yesterday? I was afraid and stammered to answer the question. But there was no excuse and I stood up gradually just tied my hands and managed to give that answer 'YES MISS'. Then she smiled and said

'You should talk to me; at least I would have given the pop-corn'. She wanted to continue but some lady teacher called her from the door side. The movement she went outside, I ran like anything to pass the urinals towards the toilet. Just came from there and had some water to settle myself in the corner bench. I thought that she would scold me; from that day I did not see her openly but in the crowd of the students, I did.

The Sports Day

The Volleyball match was going on and two teams were fighting their battle very seriously and the whole school was standing to support both the teams. Even though both were from the same school still we had perfect competitions and preferred ideologies as students were divided into houses (groups).I was also watching the match and clapping my hands as it was the ladies teams playing for finals; it was a bit interesting for teachers also.

She entered the scene and it was a great curiosity to watch her in the crowd. She just shouted 'buck up, hit it good' etc and I started watching her as there will be no more favorite for me after her entrance. As it was hot in the afternoon she was sweating and used her hand key to clean the face. Drank some water also but she cannot sustain that heat anymore and went to the staffroom. But other teachers were with the students to watch till the end.

I just went to the class to collect my water bottle and one girl was sitting there. She asked me that which team was leading and I informed about all the developments of the match. As I was about to get out of the bench holding the water bottle in my hand for my surprise; miss was near the classroom door watching me and the girl. I was a bit frightened as she moved towards me. She then started moving a bit faster towards my bench. I just said with a lot of energy 'good afternoon miss' she laughed at me and asked the water bottle. She drank the water and with that gentle smile she returned. I touched that water bottle with great enthusiasm and drank all the water so that it will not be used by anybody. I wanted to talk to her but I did not had courage apart from 'Yes Miss and No miss'. Then I thought that I should express my feelings by writing a letter sitting in the home. But we lived in a small house and there was no privacy. I planned to go to the nearby temple to my house which was not crowded in the afternoons. With a pen and a notebook I went on that day to write the letter. I prayed the God to give me all the power to write that letter. First I started 'dear miss' and scratched it and then I wrote respected miss that was bit okay. Afterwards I wrote 'you are lovely, smart, sexy' etc using my broken English. Then I wrote 'I love you miss, please miss you also love me.' Then I tarred that paper from the book and copied it and this time it was neat and there were no scratches. I kept in my pocket and the next day I carried the letter in my pocket to the school. As usual she engaged the period in the afternoon but I have planned to give this in the evening after school hours. The school bell rang and all were going home but I stood below the tree. I was just adjusting my bicycle chain to prove that it was a reason for standing there. She was moving with her books and vanity bag and but still some students were there and there was no absolute privacy. When she came near to me, she stopped and opened 'What happened?' until she finished her question, I started running with my bicycle reciting 'no miss, no miss'. My heart beat increased rapidly and after certain distance I stopped and tarred that letter into pieces; some tears started marching from my eyes; used my palm to clear my face. I did not eat any food that night; slept all the way weeping on my bed and pillow was a bit wet.

THE UNEXPRESSED LOVE

Love more and more; to live and let live

Love more and more; to create and destroy

Love more and more; to kiss and hug

Love more and more; to sing and dance

Love more and more; to marry and carry

Love more and more; to civilize and privilege

Love more and more; to express and hide

Love more and more; to meet and greet

Love more and more; to die and perish

I felt very bad when my classmate spoke openly about her sexy figure. But I was not able to tolerate and was not in a position to redefine myself in the context of a mutual relationship. I lost my mind many a times but her smile gave me the love that lasted for many years in my mind which has the power to create the waves in my mind; to write about her beauty. The dreams were so interesting that I really enjoyed a lot;

She stands on the terrace with the open hairs;

A slew less nighty; with the unwashed face

Scribbling her eyes; yawning with little sound;

Stretching her hands; to protect her eyes

from the biting sunshine;

Every day she was normal with usual sari and blouse. Usually she did not like makeup from my point of view.

Our school annual day was the special event after sports to end an academic year. My eyes were waiting to see my Goddess and then I came to know that she was busy in helping the students who were suppose to perform cultural activities. Then I made my way to a nearby classroom and saw her with the students. She was very student friendly and especially boys had all the freedom to chat with her who were our seniors. I observed that she had light red color nail polish on her fingers, lipstick just casual, some rose to her cheeks; with some shining material spotted on her face; but I came to know by my friend that someone has forced her for the development. Any way she was pretty to watch and my eyes were on a merry feast enjoying the beauty of my Goddess.

I shall hate you for making me mad in your love; for I shall love you as you were the reason to exist on this earth; be simple, be happy forever that's all I can wish

Now the exams are over and summer holidays are going on. I was playing with my area friends. But still in the evenings when I got the chance I went near the school ground and stood for hours watching the nearby boys playing cricket. I want to give life to my memories by imagining her in different situations especially in the ground. It was not easy to forget her for a second as she has become my breath. I used to write in a 100 page note book 'I Love You Miss' one page each day. It was a kind of great joy or a way to paying her respect and love.

THE DARK CHAPTER

It was a very unusual to imagine life without her during those days. So, I waited for the school to start and the first day was very special for me to meet her. I just walked into the classroom with great enthusiasm and my eyes waited for her that whole day. But she didn't come and I was depressed by that development. After waiting for a long period of two days then it was learnt by me that she has been transferred to the other school. It was a thunder blow on the small heart. That evening I did weep a lot and slept without food. I was not so matured to go and meet her in the working place.

The sea roared with the thrust; the sky cried with the pain; birds stopped singing and plants didn't move a bit; O God on mighty why did you curse me with such a worst movement in life? All the while she smiled and that was the oxygen to breathe and her absence killed me little by little; eyes burn every second to watch her; heart has stopped talking to me; mind has completely dislocated from the body; my Goddess of Beauty if you could hear me; death will not be so easy for me before I meet you; come all the way wherever you are for my survival; otherwise I am going to end this life; a lot of pressure is on me to meet you greet you and just to say ' love you miss' three simple words that are more heavy to keep them in my heart; Just come as a breeze and hug me; as a sunshine with rays that kiss my lips; as my angel who marry me in the wedding white gown; I am small and not matured, save me through your love that's all I do beg you miss.

MY PAIN

It was a great tragedy at that age I can sustain for not having either maturity or eligibility to be part of her life. It was a kind of innocence and uselessness that was supposed to happen if I would have expressed my feelings about her in front of anybody including my parents and friends.

I want to cry louder "Love you miss"; Just come to me I want to see you; with all those memories I survive; these eyes find you near the black board , near the church, in the ground and everywhere you were spotted by them. It seems impossible to survive without you every fraction of a second; dreams are still green that exposed your beauty; the smile pierces the knife in my heart whenever I remember; as you killed me with your gentle smile; just come over wherever you are? Make sure that life costs more and death nothing as it takes no time to vanish on this earth; but without you that heaven is a waste and being on earth if I can't see you; then it's a hell; now I just exist and never live; for you are the cause for me to be on this earth and you are the reason and everything that human mind can understand; you are my Monalisa; my Angel; my sweet heart; my hope and my life; Just come over to me with flying colors; enlighten that lovely gentle smile; Just give the breeze some opportunity to touch those open hairs; the nose that always give dose of energy to the men who love your glamour; lips that prove you are the special creature; Come all the way breaking all the barriers of culture; I would wait for all my life until the last breathe on this earth; I ask the clouds to tell her about my feelings; birds to convey the message; and stars to write a letter; let sun travel faster to call her with rays penetrating those remarkable eyes; God you shouldn't be so cruel to me; am I not your child?

TEARS OF BLOOD

Every fraction of a second my eyes waited for her and there was something that created sensation in my heart to recover those memories. It was not easy to get rid of those memories; so I want to cry louder and louder that she should hear and come to me.

Eyes that weep day and night; as the blood flows as tears

I had posted all the happiness into watching you in the classroom; Now what shall I do? God shouldn't have to be so cruel to me;

Heart cries louder it cannot sustain the pain;

In all my cells of the body there is an atom of your name; whom do I advise as the whole structure of body is full of your memories; as the green grass becomes dry so as became my heart; just pour some love it will start gaining rebirth; oh my angel come to me wherever you are and hug me.

I shall love you until my last breath

MY LAST WORDS TO HER

I would like to tell a story of a camel which was very close to the death. When there were just some minutes to end its life it cried 'O God provide me a sip of water, I will be thankful to you all the while' and closed its eyes. There was a heavy rain occurred during that hour in the desert. The camel enjoyed the last sip and was about to die happily but God questioned 'were you thirsty?' The camel said 'o my God; I have lived over the years and many times water has given me birth.' The camel continued that it wanted to salute the water for its nature to make living things alive many a times in their life time. God finally said 'Now are you happy ?' The camel replied ' Many rebirths was given by the water to me whenever I was thirsty and finally it was the way to thank for its nature; an honor and an occasion to salute its contribution to all the creatures of earth'.

My miss is also like water for me; She gave me rebirth with her gentle smile; She has been serving the beauty that makes human beings alive in their lives as most of them do exist but haven't they lived.

Heart cries, eyes weep and mind is blocked; wherever you are be happy; if I could meet you in my lifetime that would be the God's greatest gift to me. God bless you miss with better spouse and let every happiness come to your way as you would wish.

MISS..

Yours Lovingly

Contents